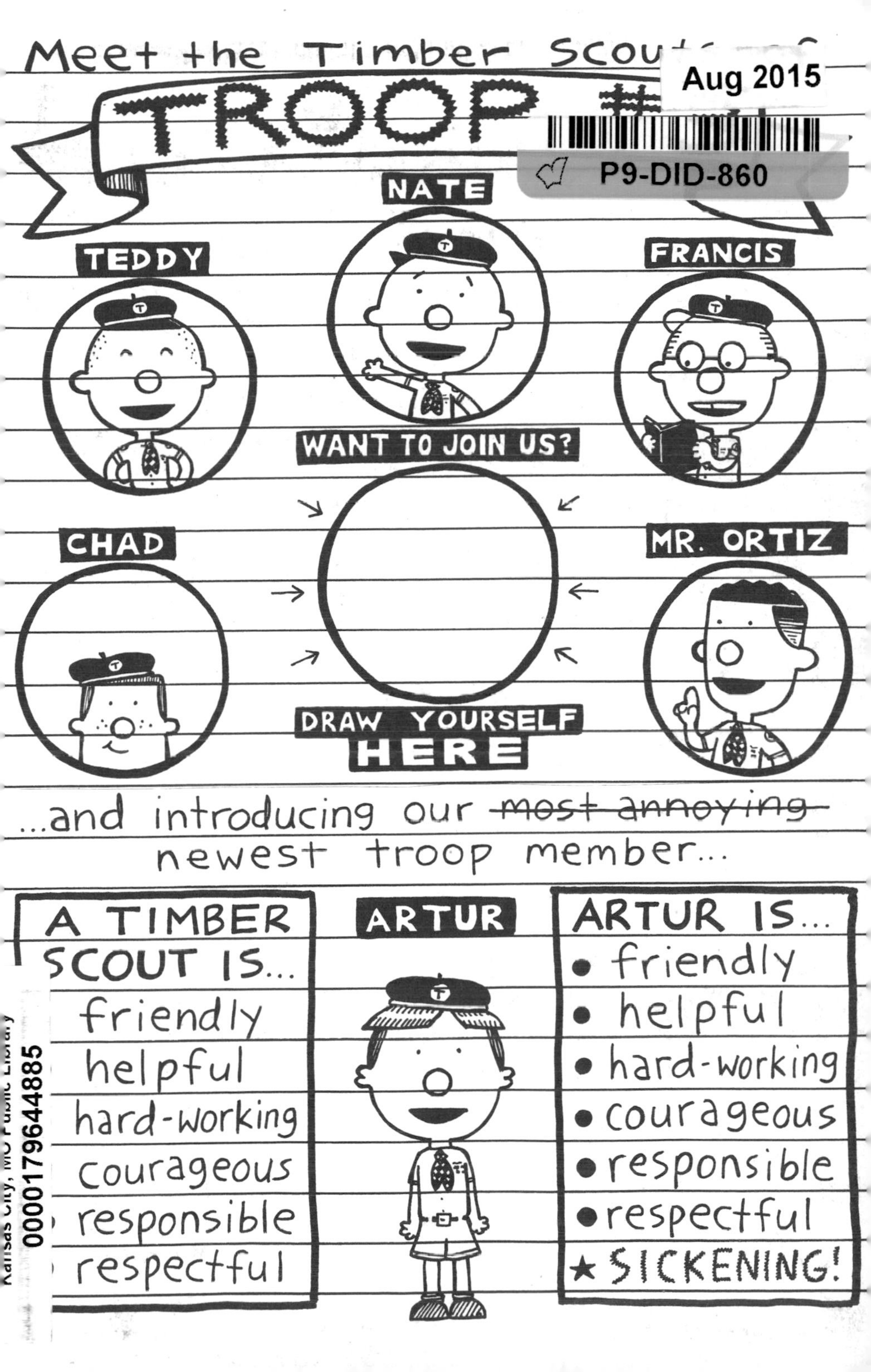
Meet the Timber Scou
TROOP #
NATE
TEDDY
FRANCIS
WANT TO JOIN US?
CHAD
MR. ORTIZ
DRAW YOURSELF HERE
...and introducing our ~~most annoying~~ newest troop member...
A TIMBER SCOUT IS...
friendly
helpful
hard-working
courageous
responsible
respectful
ARTUR
ARTUR IS...
• friendly
• helpful
• hard-working
• courageous
• responsible
• respectful
★ SICKENING!

Lincoln Peirce

HARPER
An Imprint of Harper Collins*Publishers*

Big Nate on a Roll

 For information address HarperCollins Children's Books, a division of HarperCollins Publishers, 195 Broadway, New York, NY 10007.

www.harpercollinschildrens.com
www.bignatebooks.com

Go to www.bignate.com to read the *Big Nate* comic strip.

Library of Congress Cataloging-in-Publication Data is available.
ISBN 978-0-06-194438-3 (trade bdg.)
ISBN 978-0-06-194439-0 (lib. bdg.)
ISBN 978-0-06-204744-1 (international ed.)
ISBN 978-0-06-209152-9 (Scholastic ed.)

Typography by Sasha Illingworth
14 15 16 LP/RRDH 20 19 18 17 16 15 14 13 12 11
❖
First Edition

For Dana H.P., my good one.

I never really noticed before how boring the detention room is.

I guess that's not exactly breaking news. Any room where the main activities are (1) sitting quietly with your head on the desk or (2) writing "I will not make vulgar noises during Mary Ellen Popowski's flute performance" a hundred times isn't exactly Thrillsville.

(By the way, I'm not here because I made vulgar noises during Mary Ellen Popowski's flute performance. That was last week. And it wasn't even on purpose!)

What I mean is, the room ITSELF is boring. The only things on the wall are two signs. One says QUIET, PLEASE and the other—just in case anybody's too dense to figure out sign #1—says NO TALKING. I'm not expecting them to have a TV in here or anything, but would it kill them to put up a couple of posters?

See how it took her a second to answer? She's all wrapped up in one of her cheesy romance novels.

"Can I zip down to the art studio for a sec?"

She raises an eyebrow. "The art studio? What for?"

Down goes the eyebrow. "Nate," she says, "P.S. 38 has no interest in 'jazzing up' the detention room."

"Exactly!" I answer.

Okay, so much for that idea. Guess Mrs. C.'s in one of her no-nonsense moods. Sometimes she's a little more chatty, but that's usually when it's just her and me. Today there are three other kids in here:

NAME: *Seth Quincy*
WHY HE'S HERE: *He got so mad at a bunch of kids for calling him Q-tip, he totally snapped. Personally, I think it's kind of a cool nickname, but that's just me.*

NAME: *Lee Ann Pfister*
WHY SHE'S HERE: *She broke the rule that says you can't wear shirts or blouses that show off your belly button. Not only that, she has an outie.*

NAME: *Chester Budrick*
WHY HE'S HERE: *He wanted to trade lunches with Eric Fleury, but Eric said no. So Chester stuffed a hot dog up Eric's nose. Did I mention Chester is kind of a psycho?*

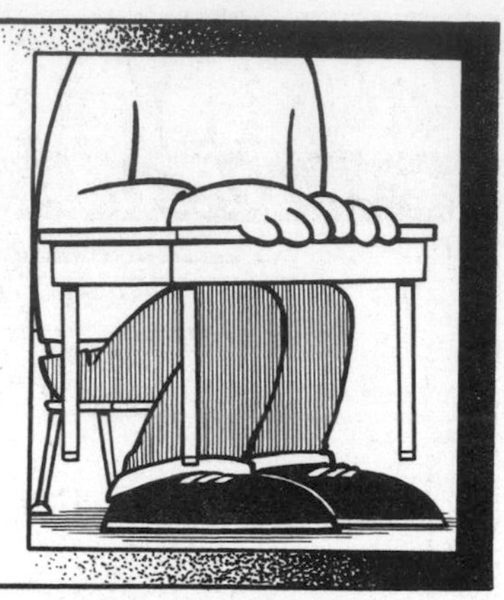

And then there's me. You probably want to know how I ended up here. Well, that makes two of us. It wasn't my fault. Not even CLOSE. It was pretty much all ARTUR'S doing. And of course I got detention while Artur, aka Mr. Lucky, got absolutely nothing! It's sort of a long story.

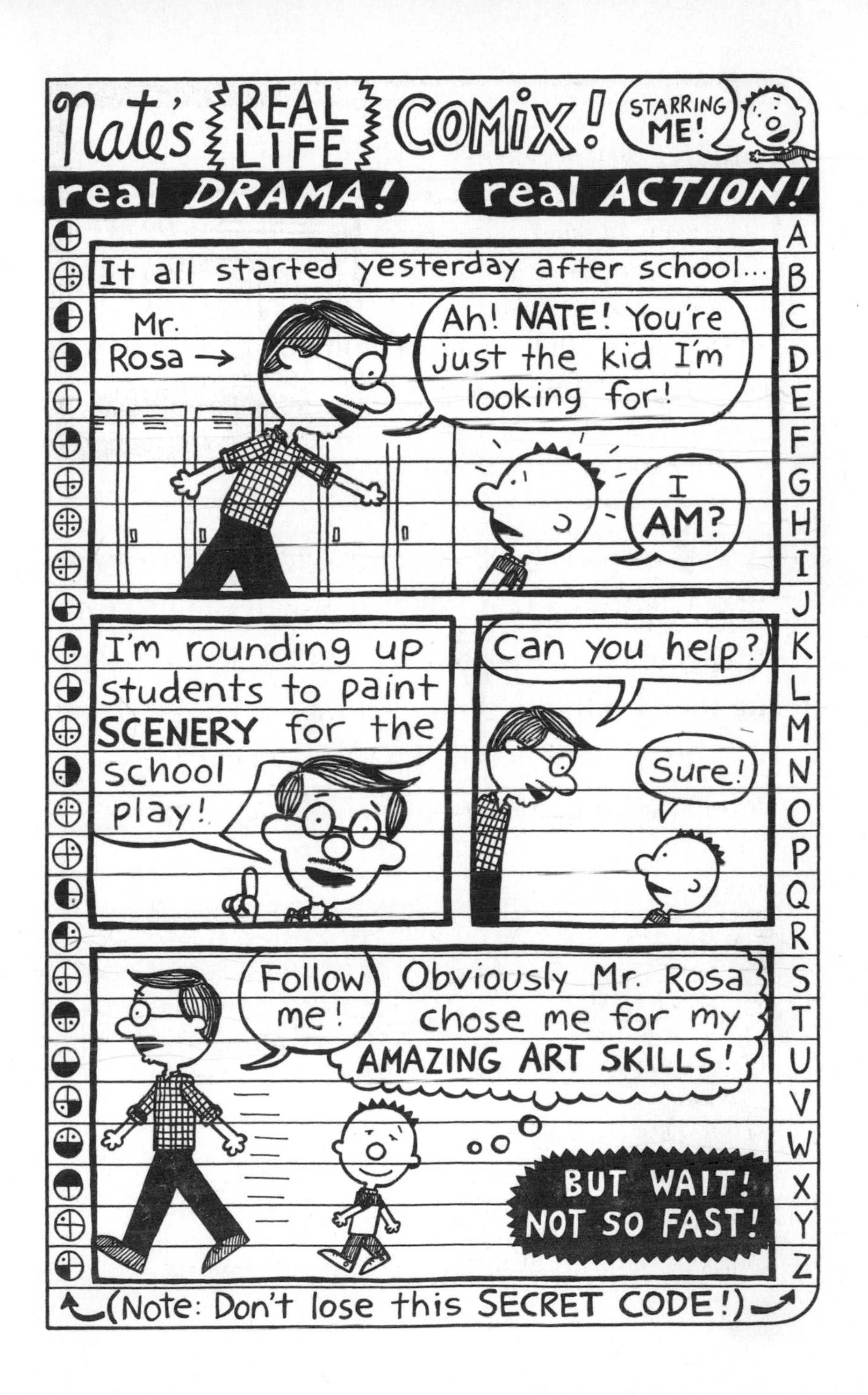
Nate's REAL LIFE COMIX!
STARRING ME!
real DRAMA! real ACTION!
It all started yesterday after school...
Mr. Rosa →
Ah! NATE! You're just the kid I'm looking for!
I AM?
I'm rounding up students to paint SCENERY for the school play!
Can you help?
Sure!
Follow me!
Obviously Mr. Rosa chose me for my AMAZING ART SKILLS!
BUT WAIT! NOT SO FAST!
A B C D E F G H I J K L M N O P Q R S T U V W X Y Z
(Note: Don't lose this SECRET CODE!)

This part of the project is a two-man job!
A two-man job? You and me?
No, I mean you and...
...ARTUR!
OMINOUS MUSIC
PAT! PAT!
! ! !
Artur, since you're so WONDERFUL, I'm going to let YOU paint the mountains and clouds!
Hokay! Thanks you very good!
Artur's "charming" broken English
BLUE

And Nate?... YOU...
Yes? YES?
... will hold the LADDER for ARTUR!
WHAT?
Hokay, Nate! I am to climbing up now!
Ooh, don't you just LOVE his cute ACCENT?
He's so DREAMY!
brush brush
This stinks.
DRIP
DRIP
HEY!

WATCH it, Artur! You're DRIPPING on me!
SUDDENLY!...
BLOOP!
GAH!
I CAN'T SEE!
stagger
stumble
YOOP!
BUMP!
CRASH!
WHAM!

GOOD HEAVENS!
ARTUR! Are you all right??
Is ARTUR all right?
Nate, YOU were SUPPOSED to be holding the LADDER!
I WAS, but...
Artur could have been badly hurt falling from such a height!
Perhaps a DETENTION will teach you a LESSON!
write write
! !
I already KNOW the lesson: ARTUR ALWAYS WINS!
THE END

It's true: He DOES always win. Let's face it, Artur has everything going for him. He's friendly, he's smart, he's good at practically everything. All the teachers love him, and so do the kids. Hey, even I like him, and I can't stand the guy.

Want to know what else is annoying? Because I got detention—which, just so we're clear on this, was thanks to Artur—I'm going to be late for my Timber Scout meeting.

Yup. I'm a scout. I used to want nothing to do with scouting, because every time Francis and Teddy came back from a Timber Scout camping trip, they always had food poisoning. Or worse.

But they finally convinced me to give it a try. It's not as dorky as I thought it might be. There are a few lame parts, but those are balanced out by the good stuff. Like the uniform. The uniform rocks.

Even the beret is kind of cool. I have to admit, before I joined the Timber Scouts, I thought the only people who wore berets were French guys and mimes.

Anyway, the stinkin' meeting's already started. Maybe I can make the second half of it. MAYBE! . . .

YES! I explode out of my chair, race down the hallway to my locker, grab my uniform, and duck into the bathroom to change. Thirty seconds later, and . . .

Teddy's dad is our troop leader, so our meetings are always at his place. It's a fifteen-minute walk from here . . .

I strap on my helmet and push off. I zip along Haywood Avenue, turn left onto Pepper Street, and start across the bridge over Beard's Creek—which really isn't a creek. It's more like a combination swamp and garbage dump.

There's a woman walking her dog up ahead. Well, maybe "dog" isn't the right word. It's one of those toy poodles that looks like somebody glued cotton balls to a weasel. I mean, if you're going to have a dog like that, why not just get a CAT?

The woman moves to her left when she hears me coming. But the dog goes the other way. Before I can slow down, her leash is stretched across the sidewalk like a trip wire, and I'm heading straight into it.

WHAM!

I sort of flip while I'm falling, so I end up landing on my backpack. That's the good news. The bad news is, my skateboard keeps going. It shoots under the bridge railing, dive-bombs into the creek . . .

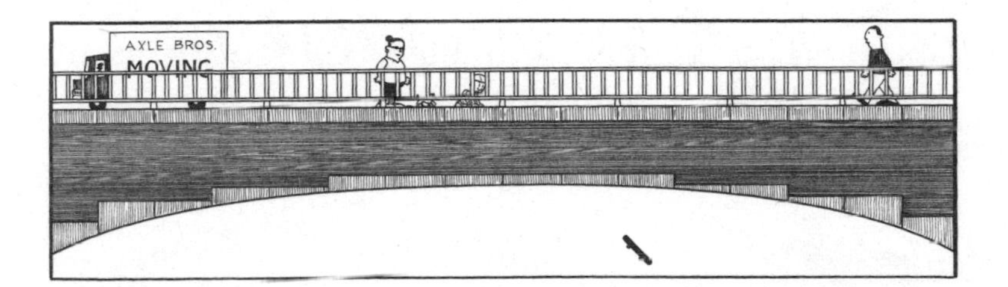

. . . and sinks into the oily water. Good-bye, skateboard.

SPLOOSH!

The dog's yapping, the woman's babbling, and people are rubbernecking as they drive by. But I can't focus on any of it. I think maybe I'm in shock. All I can do is look down at the ripples in the water where my board disappeared. Forever.

I take off my helmet in disgust and stuff it in my backpack. No more riding.

This whole disaster is one big Artur chain reaction. If he hadn't spilled paint on me, I wouldn't have (1) bumped into the ladder, (2) landed in detention, (3) been late to my

Timber Scout meeting, (4) ridden my skateboard to Teddy's house, (5) crashed into that lady and her dog, and (6) lost my board in the creek. See how it all fits together? Thanks a LOT, Artur.

It takes a while, but I finally get to Teddy's house. The guys are sitting on the front steps.

"Oh, really?" I mumble. Frankly, at this point I'm too exhausted to care.

"AND . . ." Francis says with a huge smile, "our troop has some great news!"

Great news? I perk up a little bit.

"We just initiated a new member!" Teddy announces.

Francis rattles off a fake drumroll. Teddy does his crowd noise sound effect. The door swings open, and . . .

THIS is supposed to be great news??

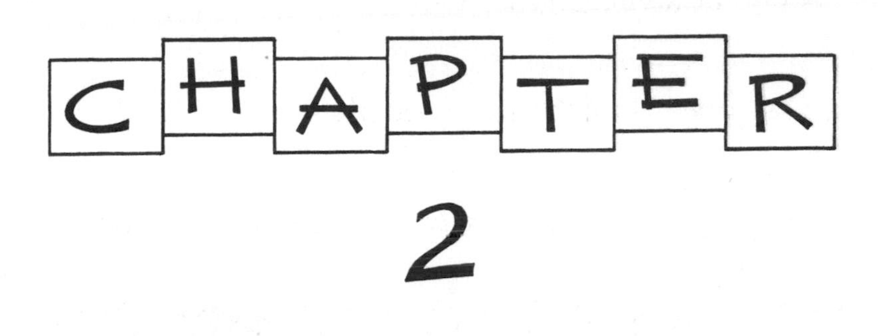

"How do I looks in my costume, guys?" he asks.

COSTUME?? It's a UNIFORM, you pinhead!

"You look awesome, Artur," says Francis.

Right. Of COURSE he looks awesome. Why WOULDN'T he? After all . . .

"How come you're making that weird face?" Teddy asks me.

"Maybe you are have gas," Artur suggests.

"I'm bummed out about missing the meeting, that's all."

Nobody says anything. Hey, fine by me. There's nothing they could say to make me feel much better, anyway.

Except THAT!

"Uh . . . hold it," says Teddy. "There actually aren't any left."

Oh, really? So Peachy McWonderful gets what should have been MINE? SHOCKER!

“Sorry,” says Teddy sheepishly.

Hey, no biggie. I’ll just starve to death, that’s all. Besides, a cookie can’t fix my REAL problem: I just blew my chance to get my attendance merit badge.

In Timber Scouts, there are merit badges for just about everything. Here are some of the ones I’ve earned so far:

HELPING HANDS - You're supposed to do good deeds without getting paid anything. So I took care of Spitsy, the dog next door, while Mr. Eustis was at a polka festival in Buffalo.
SPITSY! NO!!
NOT ON THE RUG!
GRUNT.
Turns out Spitsy had an intestinal virus that week. No wonder Mr. Eustis left town.
FIRST AID - The hardest part wasn't learning CPR, making splints, or tying a jillion tourniquets. It was practicing the Heimlich Maneuver on Chad.
Put your arms around him, Nate! Then SQUEEZE!
Teddy's dad
I'm TRYING!

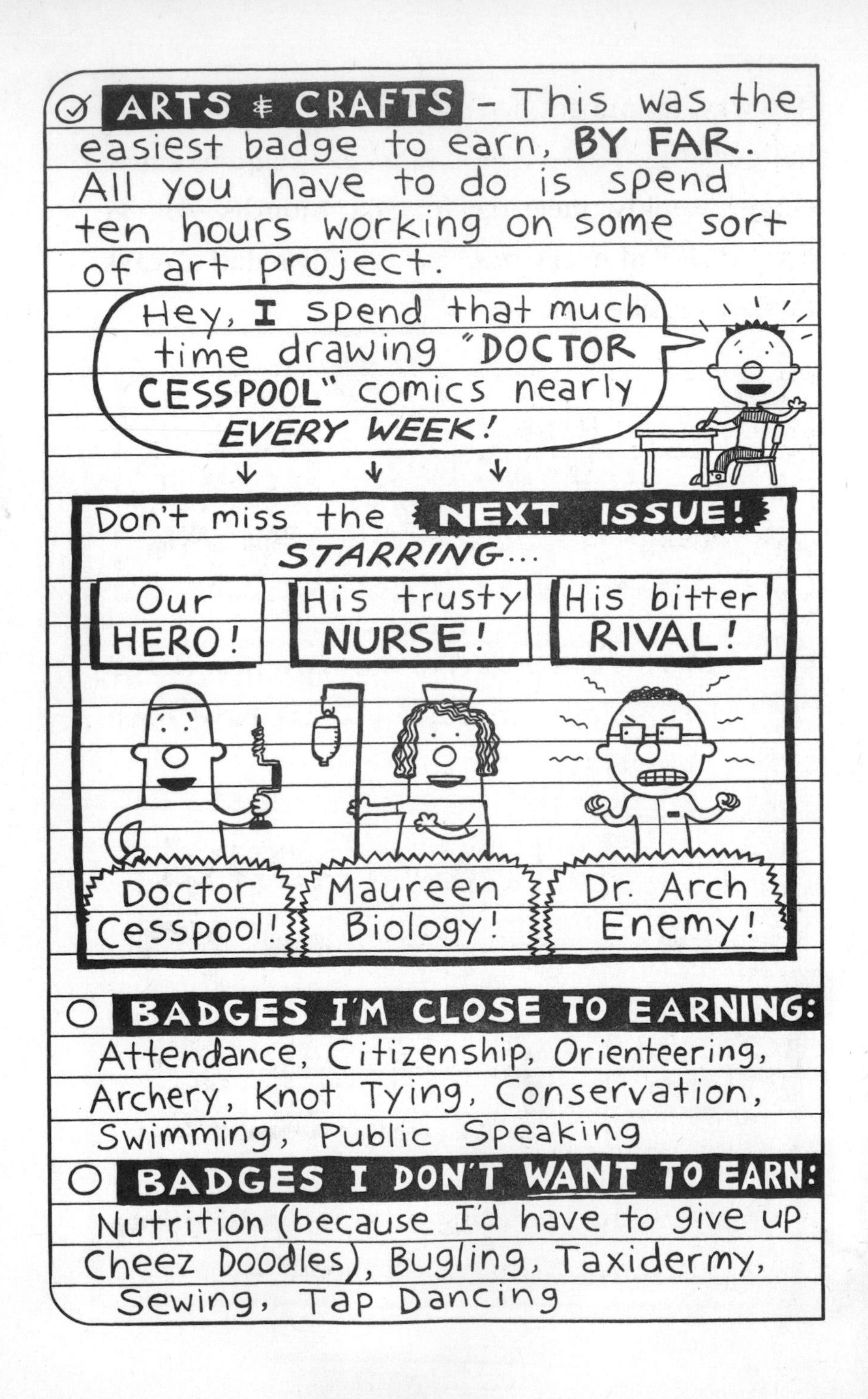
ARTS & CRAFTS - This was the easiest badge to earn, BY FAR. All you have to do is spend ten hours working on some sort of art project.
Hey, I spend that much time drawing "DOCTOR CESSPOOL" comics nearly EVERY WEEK!
Don't miss the NEXT ISSUE!
STARRING...
Our HERO!
His trusty NURSE!
His bitter RIVAL!
Doctor Cesspool!
Maureen Biology!
Dr. Arch Enemy!
BADGES I'M CLOSE TO EARNING:
Attendance, Citizenship, Orienteering, Archery, Knot Tying, Conservation, Swimming, Public Speaking
BADGES I DON'T WANT TO EARN:
Nutrition (because I'd have to give up Cheez Doodles), Bugling, Taxidermy, Sewing, Tap Dancing

Anyway, let me get back to the whole attendance badge thing. To earn one, you have to go to every single weekly meeting for six months—or at least PART of every meeting. Teddy's dad always explains it like this:

Six months is twenty-six meetings in a row. Here's the killer: Today's meeting WOULD have been number twenty-five.

"Ah!" says Artur, pointing at a car pulling into Teddy's driveway. "There is my mom!"

He motions to me and Francis. "Jump into, guys! We will give to you rides home!"

"No, thanks. I'd rather walk," I say right away. Actually, a ride would be great. If ARTUR wasn't in the car.

Good ol' Francis.

We wave good-bye to Teddy and start home. Francis lives right next to me, so it's the same trip for both of us.

“Where’s your skateboard?” he asks after a while. “Didn’t you bring it to school today?”

So much for THAT line of questioning. I’m not trying to be a jerk or anything. I just don’t feel like talking about it right now.

“Well then, how ’bout a little trivia?” Francis asks cheerfully. I groan, but it’s too late. He’s already pulled out that stupid book, and he’s flipping through it with sort of a crazed look in his eyes.

FRANCIS FACT:
He has a book called “Fact-tastic Trivia” that he carries with him at all times.

"Ready?" he asks.

"Nope," I answer. Hey, I've got to be honest.

"Try another question," I say. "That one's too easy."

"Okay," he says, clearing his throat. "What astrophysicist was responsible for—?"

"I was KIDDING, Einstein," I tell him.

"Well, mostly we talked about our fund-raiser," he says.

"They're wall hangings with little sayings on them," he explains. "Take a look."

He hands me a brochure. I scan the page. Wait, is this a JOKE?

"They are pretty bad," Francis admits.

I'M A NUT!
DON'T YOU LOVE...
GRANDMAS?
HANG IN THERE!
FOLLOW YOUR RAINBOW!
SHARING...
IS CARING!
"SEAL" OF APPROVAL
WHO, ME?
I NEED A HUG!

I've sold stuff door-to-door before, but never anything THIS lame. This Warm Fuzzies thing is going to end up somewhere on my list of . . .

3 RAFFLE TICKETS FOR LITTLE LEAGUE
HEY! YOU'RE the kid who rode his bike through my FLOWER BEDS!!
2 SCENTED CANDLES FOR THE SOCCER BOOSTERS
AACK! I'M ALLERGIC TO WAX!
CALL 911!
"ocean mist"
1 MAGAZINES FOR THE CHESS TEAM (Note: Always find out where your teachers live BEFORE you ring any doorbells!)
NO, I don't want a subscription to "Skydiving Weekly"!
But as long as you're HERE, come in for some TUTORING!
WORSE
HORRIBLE
NIGHTMARE
TOTAL

"How come we have to do a fund-raiser, anyway?" I grumble.

"That's just for the cost of our uniforms," explains Francis. "We need extra money to upgrade our camping gear."

I snort. "We won't raise much selling THIS junk."

Francis frowns. "You'll need a better sales pitch than THAT," he says, "if you want to win one of the prizes."

"There's a first, second, and third place prize for the scouts who sell the most wall hangings," he explains patiently. "And they're GOOD prizes, too, because this fund-raiser isn't just for OUR troop! . . ."

Francis jumps. "My alarm!" he says.

"Wait! Francis! What are the prizes?"

"They're on the back of the brochure I gave you!" he calls over his shoulder. "I'll see you later!"

I flip the brochure over.

A build-your-own-robot kit? Not really my thing, unless the robot can do my social studies homework for me.

No, thanks. Telescopes are a total rip-off. They're always like: "Explore the galaxy!" But when you actually look through them, all you can see is a reflection of your eyeball.

And the GRAND prize is . . .

A blast of energy shoots through me. Suddenly, selling those lame wall hangings seems a lot more interesting. Now there's a GOAL to work toward. Now I'm MOTIVATED.

For a prize like THIS, I'll sell ANYTHING!

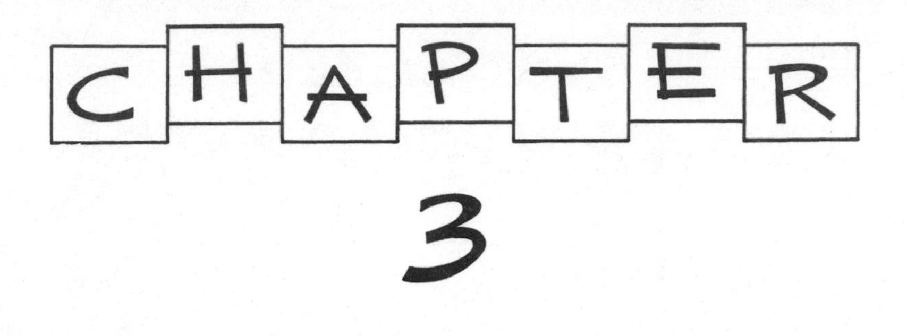

"Prepare to finish second, guys!" I announce the next morning when I meet Francis and Teddy for the walk to school.

"Wait a minute," says Francis. "Yesterday all you could talk about was how LAME those things were!"

"They ARE lame," I say.

Francis gives me one of his looks. "Uh, and what's the 'Nate Wright charm,' exactly?"

"That's a question MANY have asked," Teddy says.

"You clowns wouldn't know charm if it hit you on the head," I say.

Which, come to think of it, sounds like a pretty good idea!

"Hey, it isn't me or Teddy you have to worry about," says Francis.

"Artur?" I repeat. "What do you mean?"

"He seemed pretty psyched about the fund-raiser at our meeting yesterday," Francis explains.

"Yeah," agrees Teddy. "He really wants to win that skateboard."

Skateboard? MY skateboard??

"I bet Artur's a good salesman," Francis says.

Great. I can picture it now.

Maybe I'm exaggerating, but not by much. Grown-ups tend to get all gushy whenever Artur's around, and I'll tell you why: He's always sucking up to them.

See? Artur's all deep in conversation with Mr. Galvin, who's not exactly Captain Charisma. Why would anyone talk to Mr. Galvin if they didn't HAVE to? Artur's the biggest suck-up in P.S. 38.

MR. GALVIN FACT:
He has a collection of potatoes shaped like famous scientists.

Correction: Artur's the SECOND biggest suck-up in P.S. 38. GINA's ahead of him.

Here's what bugs me: It WORKS. The sucking up, I mean. The teachers fall for it every time. They're always like: Artur's so THIS. Gina's so THAT. Artur and Gina. Gina and Artur.

Wait. Whoa. WOW!

I just got such a great idea, it almost blew my pants off!

Why didn't I think of it BEFORE? The two of them are so alike. They're king and queen of the honor roll, they never get in trouble, and they're both a total pain in my butt. So what are we WAITING for? Let's get these two lovebirds TOGETHER!

There's only one teensy little problem:

Artur's already going out with Jenny.

Don't ask me why. Everybody with half a brain knows that I'D be a much better match for Jenny than Artur. When you do a comparison, it's not even CLOSE.

NATE (YAY!)	VS. Artur (YAWN.)
• Ruggedly handsome	• Unruggedly wimpy
• Hair is stylish and spiky	• Hair is flat and stringy
Aura of Confidence	Aura of Cauliflower
Beef-cake!	Cup-cake!
• Super athlete (soccer, baseball, etc.)	• Takes ballroom dancing lessons
• "Street" smart	• "Book" smart
• Hilarious sense of humor	• Doesn't understand knock-knock jokes
• Born to be wild	• Born to be mild

Plus, I've known Jenny WAY longer than ARTUR has. She was just about to start liking me, and then HE had to move to town. It's an OUTRAGE!

But back to my brilliant idea: What if I can convince Artur that he and Gina are soul mates? Then he'll dump Jenny . . .

Oof. Pancaked by my own locker. That's a little embarrassing. Good thing Jenny's not around to see this.

"Nate," says a voice.

Oh, really? Thanks for pointing that out, Artur. That's so OBSERVANT of you!

I shove everything back in place and make it to homeroom on time. That's key, because I

can't afford to get detention. Not today. I need to be free after school . . .

So I turn myself into Johnny B. Good Behavior. When Mrs Godfrey needs a volunteer, I raise my hand. When Ms. Clarke asks a question, I answer.

When Mr. Staples tells one of his lame jokes, I laugh. Basically, I spend the whole day acting just like Artur.

I hate myself.

But it works. I make it to science, my last class of the day, without getting a single detention. Only forty-five minutes to go.

Mr. Galvin launches into one of his drone-athons, and I can feel my brain switch to autopilot. I can't stop thinking about that grand prize skateboard. It's WAY nicer than the one I lost in the creek.

I bet it's worth ten times as much. And it's CUSTOMIZED!

I hear something behind me. I turn around, and there's Gina peering over my shoulder. I slam the notebook shut,

but it's too late. She shoots her hand into the air in triumph.

I stare at Gina in disbelief. But why am I surprised? This is what she lives for. She shoots me an evil little grin.

"Bring me your notebook, Nate," Mr. Galvin says.

Young man. When they call you young man, it's pretty much a guarantee that you're getting detention. Unless you come up with a miracle. Unless you try something completely crazy.

Like the truth.

"Just a moment," Mr. Galvin cuts in. He gets up from his desk.

I swallow hard. How could telling the truth make things WORSE? Everybody's staring and whispering as I follow Mr. Galvin out of the classroom. The sound of the closing door echoes down the hallway. What's he going to do to me?

For the longest time, he doesn't do ANYthing. My ears are burning. My palms are slick with sweat. Finally, he clears his throat.

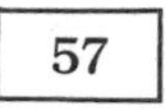

"Young man," Mr. Galvin says seriously, "you and I are going to have a little talk . . ."

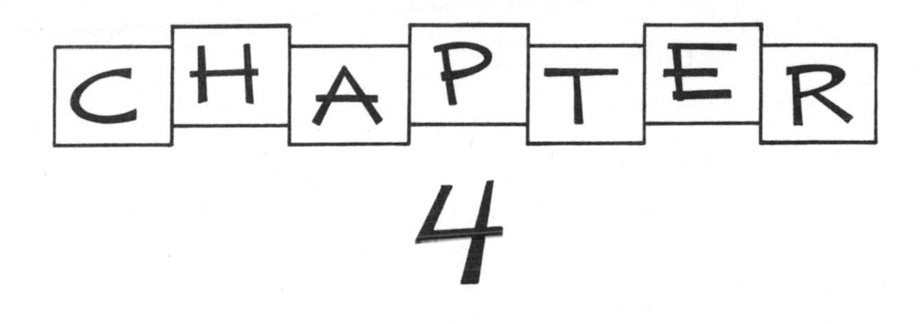

CHAPTER 4

"You DID say you're a scout, didn't you?"

Where's he going with this? "Uh-huh," I answer nervously. "A Timber Scout."

"Yes sir," I say quickly.

"I'm going to let you in on a little secret, Nate," Mr. Galvin says. Wait, is he . . . SMILING?? Old Fossil Face NEVER smiles. Or maybe his dentures are slipping again. Either way, it's kind of creepy.

Whoops. I probably shouldn't have sounded so shocked. But it's sort of hard to believe that Mr. Galvin was ever a scout. Or a kid.

"We had to raise money back in MY day, too," he continues.

Believe it? Dude, I don't even know what a galosh IS.

"Now listen, Nate," he says, and suddenly he's Joe Serious again. "I don't approve of drawing during class . . ."

Really? Wow, this is like one of those stupid TV movies, where all of a sudden I realize:

. . . and then he says:

But exactly three and a half seconds later . . .

Okay, so I guess this ISN'T like one of those TV movies after all. I'd better get back to my desk and pretend to look busy. The NICE Mr. Galvin just disappeared. Say hello to his evil twin.

The day ends with a bang: I tell Gina that I didn't get detention after all. HA!

And speaking of Gina . . . remember my idea? The one about Gina and Artur getting together?

"Ah!" says Artur. "Hallo, Nate!"

Yeah, hallo yourself. Enough small talk. "Listen, Artur, ol' buddy," I say.

"Eh?" says Artur. "What abouts her?"

"Well . . . she's pretty nice, don't you think?"

Artur looks confused. "Why are you say?" he asks.

Come on, Artur, WORK with me. I can't make you and Gina a couple with THAT attitude. "She's got a lot going for her," I tell him. "She's smart, she's . . . ummmm . . . let's see here . . . she's . . ."

Sorry. Had something stuck in my throat for a sec.

Artur nods. "Hmm," he says. "Yes, I thinks I know what you are try to say."

You DO? Wow, I must be more convincing than I thought! Could Artur actually FALL for this??

I'm about to seal the deal when . . .

Sailing? Excellent! If Artur's stuck on a BOAT somewhere, he won't be doing any FUND-RAISING! I remember what Francis said this morning:

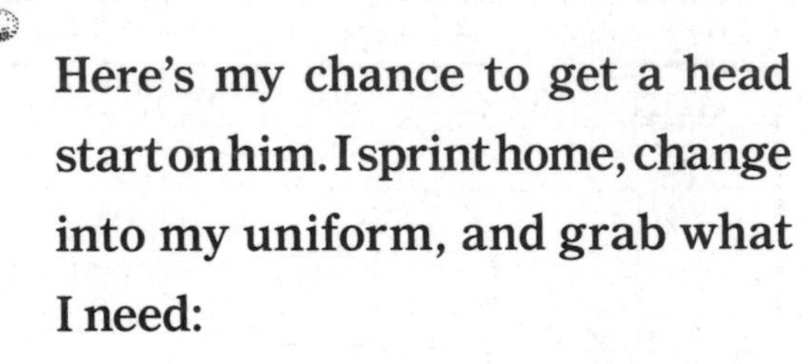

Here's my chance to get a head start on him. I sprint home, change into my uniform, and grab what I need:

And then there's my secret weapon: I'm a Timber Scout! People can't resist a man in uniform. Who wouldn't want to help a bunch of scouts buy some new camping gear?

I just hope our next camping trip is better than the LAST one.

And so...
Mount Nicnack State Park
Okay, gang, I'LL lead one group...
...and NATE'S DAD will lead the other!
Hi, kids!
I ♡ NATURE!
Okay, scouts, LET'S CLIMB!
SUMMIT
GOSH, this is a steep mountain!
We're not even ON the mountain yet!
This is the ACCESS TRAIL from the PARKING LOT!
Right. I knew that.
I ♡ NATURE

EVENTUALLY...
Where've you BEEN? We reached the top an HOUR ago!
We had to keep stopping so Nate's dad could rest.
WHEEZE! GASP!
What a VIEW!
Can I have the binoculars, Dad?
Oops. I think I left them in the car.
SMAK!
Follow me, men! This trail leads to our campsite!
HUP!... TWO!... THREE!... FOUR!

LATER...
Sorry I slowed us down by falling in the river!
Twice.
We'll build a campfire so you can warm up!
HOP TO IT, GANG!
It's getting dark!
Let's set up the tents!
GRRZZZOWLL!
WHAT WAS THAT??
GRRRZZZONNNK!
It's a WOLF!
It's a BEAR!
Relax, fellas, RELAX!

It's just NATE'S DAD!
GZZRR!
Next day...
Ah, nothing like a breakfast of TRAIL MIX!
crunch
munch
slurp
Well, HI there, li'l possum! Want some trail mix?
DAD! THAT'S NOT A POSSUM!
Yip!
skunk
FSSSST!

And we all lived skunkily ever after. Or at least for the rest of that day. It takes a long time to get the stench off. After that, I made Dad promise never to be a parent volunteer again.

I head for Mr. Eustis's house. He probably THINKS he doesn't need one of these cheeseball wall hangings. But I'll convince him. Just wait 'til he hears my sales pitch.

"Sorry about that, Nate," says Mr. Eustis, running over. "You know how much Spitsy likes you!"

Yeah? Well, he also likes chasing trees and licking himself for hours at a time. So excuse me if I'm not exactly flattered.

"Were you looking for me?" Mr. Eustis asks.

Turns out, Mr. Eustis is a soft touch. Maybe it's because he feels bad that Spitsy used me as a tackling dummy, but he buys a wall hanging.

I write his name and address on my clipboard. That's eight bucks for the Timber Scouts. And more important . . .

After that it gets harder. For some reason, a lot of people aren't home at four o'clock. And the ones who ARE home have already bought stuff to support the track team, the Dungeons & Dragons Club, or the Left-Handed Needlepoint Society.

And some people are just flat-out weird.

But I plug away. After a couple of hours, I've sold five Warm Fuzzies. That's forty bucks!

I do some quick math. We've got a two-week selling period. If I sell five of these things every day for two weeks . . .

Did I mention how much I hate math?

The point is, if I can keep up this pace, I'll raise a ton of money for the Timber Scouts. AND I'll be WAY ahead of . . .

ARTUR!
WARM FUZZIES

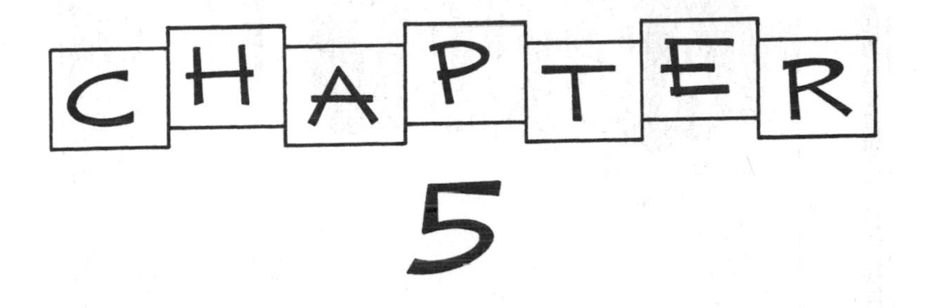

He sees me coming up the driveway. MY driveway.

Is he for real? What does he expect me to do—give him the Timber Scout secret handshake? Not that we HAVE a secret handshake. And by the way, what's he even DOING here?

He looks puzzled. "Yes, EXACT," he says. "Just like YOU, I am doing, Nate. Sailing wall hangings."

Sailing? SAILING??

"Ah!" he says. "Yes! SELLing."

Oh, brother. Here I was thinking Artur was cruising around on a LAKE somewhere, and he's been out selling Warm Fuzzies to my DAD! What a dirty trick.

"I am go home now," he says. "So longs, Nate."

"Wait just a sec, Artur."

I have to ask. I don't want to know, really. It's more like I NEED to know.

"Oh, not a lots," he says with a wave.

Twenty? Did he say TWENTY?? That's IMPOSSIBLE! Nobody could sell twenty of those stupid wall hangings in two hours!

And then Dad walks up behind me.

I'll say this for the guy: His timing's incredible. Somehow, he always finds the very worst moment to make some amazingly boneheaded comment.

So here I am, ALREADY in a bad mood because his royal highness has sold FOUR TIMES the number of Warm Fuzzies that I have . . . and Dad drops this little bomb on me:

That does it. Tommy Tactless just pressed the wrong button. Stand back and cover your ears, everybody. I'm about to let Dad have it.

Except Dad's not done. "It was so thoughtful of him to bring those brownies," he says.

Huh? "Brownies?"

"He told me you missed out on the snack at your troop meeting yesterday," Dad explains.

I don't get it. "Didn't Artur try to sell you any wall hangings?" I ask.

"What? Of COURSE not," says Dad. He seems a little taken aback. "Why would he do that?"

I think about it. I guess Dad's right. Artur WOULDN'T do that.

Anyway, at least I don't have to yell at Dad now. Which is good, because if I yelled at him, he'd probably ground me.

Remember when I mentioned the school play? This year the Drama Club's doing "Peter Pan," and tonight is opening night. Francis, Teddy, and I are going together.

I'm pretty psyched to check it out, actually, because I've only seen "Peter Pan" once in my life. Dad took me and Ellen to some sort of community theater production. I was only in second grade, so some of the details are kind of sketchy. But here's what I remember about . . .

When the actors were flying around their bedroom, it was so OBVIOUS it was fake. YOU COULD SEE THE WIRES!!
I'LL GET YOU, PETER PAN!
According to the program, the guy playing Captain Hook was an expert clarinet player. So I'm guessing his hook wasn't real.
Ellen spent the whole night LECTURING me. Who died and made HER Miss Theater Authority?
It's called "INTERMISSION," not "HALFTIME."
POP CORN

I got a really bad gas bubble and had to go to the men's room. I was in there forever. So I totally missed a huge chunk of the play.
CLAP!
CLAP!
Rats.
During the big sword fight scene, Captain Hook's sword snapped in half, which you could tell wasn't supposed to happen. So then somebody threw a new sword on-stage, and Captain Hook caught it in midair and kept fighting. And then the crowd went wild, and Dad said:
CRAK!
The show must go on!

An hour later I meet Francis and Teddy at our regular spot, and we head over to school.

"Good thing we bought our tickets in advance," Francis says.

" . . . have you guys sold any wall hangings yet?"

"Five," I say.

"Wow, I only sold ONE, and that was to my grandmother!" says Francis. "Five's GOOD, Nate!"

"I know—isn't that sick?" I say. "Winning that skateboard is going to be harder than I thought."

"Well, if you don't win," Teddy points out, "at least you already have a nice board."

"Uh . . . not exactly," I say, and I tell them my horror story of the poodle, the bridge, and the skydiving skateboard. They react just how you'd expect your two best friends to react.

Francis pulls himself together. "Sorry," he says unconvincingly. "It really isn't funny."

"Not at all," Teddy agrees, chuckling.

"Then it's got something in common with YOU two morons," I say.

The cafetorium's already packed when we get there. "You guys go find us some seats," I tell Francis and Teddy. "I'll grab some programs."

What LUCK! She's ALONE! Artur, the amazing Velcro Boy, is nowhere in sight! I wonder if . . . HEY!

Maybe my little talk with Artur about GINA is starting to sink in! Maybe he picked up the phone, called Jenny, and said:

And if there IS trouble in paradise, I bet Jenny's really bummed out, right? She's going to need some cheering up . . . from Yours Truly!

Boy, what a buzzkill. Just as I'm about to say hi to Jenny, Mr. Wonderful swoops in with his diploma from charm school, flashing his sappy smile and wearing his scout uniform . . .

Wait a minute. Scout uniform?

Why is Artur wearing his uniform to the school play? That's just plain weird.

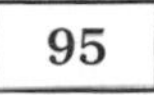

But there's no time to think about that now. They're dimming the lights. The play's starting.

And it's a good play, too. The only thing that goes wrong in Act One is when Michael (aka Chad) almost destroys the set during his flying scene. But frankly, that just makes it more entertaining.

Intermission comes along really fast. The lights go on, and we get up to stretch our legs.

“Let’s get something to eat,” Teddy says.

We go out the door and around the corner. Suddenly Francis stops short.

“Guys!” he says, surprised. “Check THIS out!”

I stare across the crowded lobby. My stomach sinks into my socks. I can’t believe what I’m seeing. Now I get it. Now I know why Artur wore his scout uniform tonight.

Forget about the snack.

I just lost my appetite.

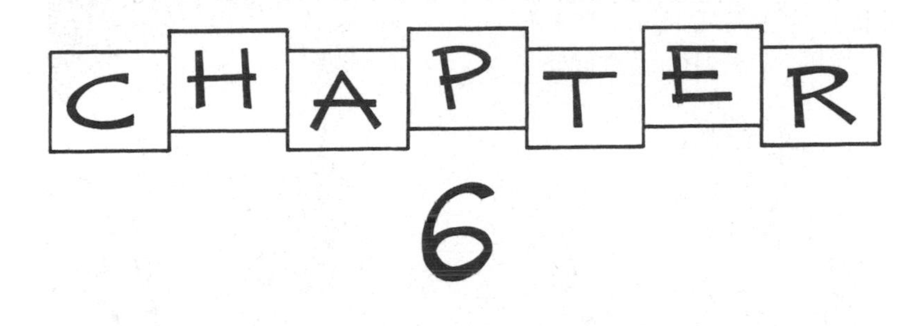

Chapter 6

The rest of the play is kind of a blur. I can't stop thinking about Artur.

Well, as long as I'm in a poetic mood, I might as well go with it. How about THIS one:

Or maybe . . .

I write a few more poems about Artur in my head during the walk home. It helps me block out all the stuff Teddy and Francis are saying.

Okay, guys, I get it. Feel free to stop talking.

This really stinks out loud. Artur's been a Timber Scout for ONE DAY! How come HE gets to sell wall hangings at the play? Why does HE get special privileges?

Now he's even FURTHER ahead of me. He probably thinks he's won that skateboard already.

I am NOT going to roll over and let Artur beat me. I bet I can sell enough Warm Fuzzies to catch up to him. There's GOT to be a way!

And there it is! I mean, there SHE is.

Ellen has a part-time job at Daffy Burger. That explains why she's dressed like a ventriloquist's dummy. AND that pile of cash on the table.

"Have I got a deal for YOU!" I say, waving the brochure under her big ol' nose.

“I don’t want to redecorate my room,” she says flatly. “I like my room how it is.”

Right. All those stuffed animals and teen idol posters? Classy, Ellen. Real classy.

I keep trying. Begging, actually. “It’s for a great cause,” I remind her. “Pleeeeeeeease?”

She gives one of those dramatic sighs. You’d think I just asked her to donate a kidney or something.

"Excellent choice," I say, even though the unicorn is the butt ugliest one there is. "And what else?"

Her eyes narrow. "ExCUSE me?" she says.

"I was . . . uh . . . hoping you'd buy more than one," I tell her. "Maybe three . . . or four . . ."

She snatches her money off the table. "Dream ON, Nate!" she snaps. "If you want to sell THAT many of your little wall hangings . . ."

Buy them myself. Gee, thanks, Ellen. That's about as helpful as a fart in a bathtub. That's . . . that's . . .

Let me rephrase that: I'M brilliant. My amazing brain just thought of a way to win that skateboard!

And I'll only have to sell those stupid Warm Fuzzies to one person:

Can you guess how I'm going to pull this off? Hang on while I grab a pencil and paper . . .

FACT #2: There are TONS of ways to raise money for YOURSELF!
BONK!
50¢
YARD WORK
LEMONADE STAND
BABY-SITTING
Now let's do the math and COMBINE these two facts!
Did somebody mention MATH?
Mr. Staples
FACT #1
+ FACT #2
= FACT #3: I'll spend the next two weeks earning as much money as I can...
... then use ALL of it to buy WALL HANGINGS!
"Warm Fuzzies"

See how it works? This way, I don't have to waste my time trying to sell people something they don't want! I can earn money however I FEEL like it!

"Did you have fun at the play?"

"Yeah, it was good," I say. Except for the Artur thing. But I don't mention that. Dad wouldn't get it.

"I'd be happy to buy a couple of these if it would help your scout troop," he says.

"Thanks, Dad, but you don't have to," I tell him.

He gives me a look like he doesn't quite believe me. I'm used to that. When you're a genius like I am, it comes with the territory.

"Okay, well, good night, then," he says. "And don't stay up drawing comics, okay? It's late."

He's right, it IS pretty late. But I never go to sleep without drawing comics. It's part of my bedtime routine. It's like flossing, except it's more fun. And it doesn't make my gums bleed.

ULTRA-NATE
SUPER 6TH GRADER!
One fine day...
I like to riding bikes!
Me, too!
Artur→
Jenny→
CAUTION! STEEP HILL!
SUDDENLY...
What the...?
KLIK! KLIK!
MY BRAKES DON'T WORK!
KLIK! KLIK!
DO something, Artur!
I can't. Because even though peoples thinks I am perfect, I am actual a wussy boy.
HELP!
?

Meanwhile...
Thank you for helping me across the street, young man!
Aw, shucks!
HELP!!
That's JENNY'S voice!
super sharp hearing
THIS is a job...
...for ULTRA-NATE!
RRRIP!
I'll ride to the rescue on my NATEBOARD!
ZOW!
WILL ULTRA-NATE GET THERE IN TIME?
YAAAAAH!
HONK!
runaway truck

NAB!
HONK!
YOU SAVED MY LIFE!
Just doing my job!
JENNY! You are HOKAY!
YES, no thanks to YOU!
BYE, Artur! ULTRA-NATE's my boyfriend from now on!
Nobody can compete with ULTRA-NATE!
Especially a nobody like YOU!
THE END

The next morning's Saturday, but am I sleeping in? Not a chance.

"Nate," says Dad when I go downstairs, "will you please take these letters out to the mailbox?"

Oops. Mistake. Dad gives me the Hairy Eyeball.

"Never mind," I say quickly. "I'll do it for free."

"How generous of you," he says, still glaring at me as I scoot outside.

Okay, maybe I got a little greedy there. But how ELSE am I supposed to catch up with Artur? I've got to be on the lookout for any chance to make money.

"Oh, just a sprained knee," he says. "I've got to take it easy for a few days, that's all."

Hear that?

Opportunity is knocking!

"So you'll need someone to walk Spitsy!" I point out.

"That's right," he answers.

We make a deal: Mr. Eustis agrees to pay me eight dollars a day for walking Spitsy all week. That's enough to buy seven Warm Fuzzies!

"You can start right now," he says, handing me Spitsy's leash. "But be careful, Nate . . ."

"Don't worry, Mr. Eustis," I say confidently. "We're only walking to the park and back."

CHAPTER 7

Everything. THAT'S what could go wrong . . .

I'm not just talking about walking Spitsy. The whole WEEKEND was a disaster. Sure, I made a little money, so I'm happy about that. I guess.

It started out fine.

Spitsy and I headed for the park.

I thought dogs were supposed to have some sort of built-in GPS, but not Spitsy. He couldn't find his way out of a paper bag. And that's just ONE of the reasons he's a total failure as a dog. Here are a few others:

3 He gets bullied by the neighborhood squirrels.
NYUK! NYUK! NYUK!
I'm embarrassed for you.
2 He comes over to our house all the time to watch lame TV shows with Ellen.
Welcome back to "Wide World Of Cheerleading"!
1 HE LIKES CATS!!!
Sigh...
Z
PURRRRR

Anyway, I saw right away why Mr. Eustis called Spitsy unpredictable. He kept zigzagging all over the place. A couple of times he almost yanked the leash out of my hand.

So I tied it to my belt.

A belt-leash combo! It sure seemed like a good idea at the time. Maybe even a MONEYMAKING idea. There must be lots of dog owners out there who'd pay for a quality product like this.

Then Spitsy saw Pickles.

Pickles is Francis's cat. I'm no cat expert—I HATE cats—but I know there are two kinds: indoor and outdoor. Pickles is an outdoor cat. She acts like she owns the neighborhood, lying around in random driveways and giving everybody the evil eye. She's totally obnoxious.

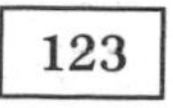

You know what else she is? Spitsy's girlfriend. At least SPITSY thinks so. Whenever he sees her, look out. He goes from zero to crazy in no time flat.

He took off. And I was right behind him. With that leash tying us together like a couple of escaped convicts, I didn't exactly have a choice.

What is it with me and dog leashes lately? That one on the bridge cost me my skateboard. And THIS one nearly KILLED me.

Want some advice? Don't run into a tree at full speed. One of you is going to end up with a headache. And it won't be the tree.

Of course the leash came loose. Spitsy took off. And guess who had to spend an hour tracking down the happy couple.

And then, when I finally dragged Spitsy back home, I had to deal with Dad. Or, as I like to call him . . .

Dad overreacts to everything. So when he saw my

eye swelling up like a soccer ball, of course he was POSITIVE I had a concussion.

I didn't. But we wasted two hours going to the emergency room just so some doctor could shine a flashlight in my eyes and say:

Great. So instead of making money to keep up with Artur, I was stuck on the couch, holding a bag of frozen peas on my face. What a waste of a Saturday.

But I still had Sunday . . . AND a guaranteed fool-proof plan. I got up super early and spent an hour cranking out some eye-catching business cards.

Before anyone was awake, I went all over the neighborhood, sticking cards in doors and on windshields.

Then I went home and waited for the phone to ring.

AND IT DID!!!

Not just once. It rang OFF THE HOOK. Mrs. McNulty hired me to weed her garden. The Petersons asked me to move some boxes into their basement. And when Mr. Eustis saw my black eye—hello, guilt trip!—he paid me to paint the railing on his front steps.

By midafternoon, I'd already earned almost FIFTY DOLLARS! Business was booming. Everything was going great.

And then . . .

It was that lady who just moved into the Nelsons' old house.

"Yup!" I told her. "That's my business card!"

"Well, I have a job for you, if you're available."

Another customer!! That meant another chance to catch up to Artur. I was gaining on him. One odd job at a time.

But this wasn't just an odd job.

This was BIZARRE.

At least two dozen ceramic lawn gnomes were grouped together by the porch. It looked like a coffee break at Santa's workshop.

"My friends and I need your help," the lady said.

Uh . . . friends? There was nobody else in the yard. Then I realized she was talking about the gnomes.

"Just move each gnome to the flag that matches his name," she instructed me cheerfully.

Yikes. It was already pretty weird that she had enough lawn gnomes to start her own football team. But she gave them NAMES? This lady was definitely a few slices short of a loaf.

"I'll pay you twenty-five dollars," she said as she went inside.

That was good money. But it wasn't EASY money. Those gnomes were heavier than they looked. And, to be honest, they creeped me out a little bit. Maybe it was all those rosy cheeks. Maybe it was the stupid names like Cheeky, Krinkles, and Sir Potbelly. Whatever. I was halfway done when . . .

Kevin is Captain Hook in "Peter Pan." He was on his way to the show. And he had his sword with him.

"It's just wood with silver paint," he said, handing it to me. "Be careful with it—the handle's a little loose."

"Hey!" Kevin yelled. "Nate, LOOK OUT!"

I WAS looking out. I THOUGHT I was, anyway. The sword wasn't anywhere close to the gnome in front of me.

The gnome behind me wasn't quite so lucky.

Kevin grabbed the sword back from me and checked it for damage. "Are you DEAF or just STUPID?" he shouted angrily. "I TOLD you to be CAREFUL!"

He stalked off, shooting me a nasty look over his shoulder.

"SORRY, Kevin!" I called after him. "I guess I just . . ."

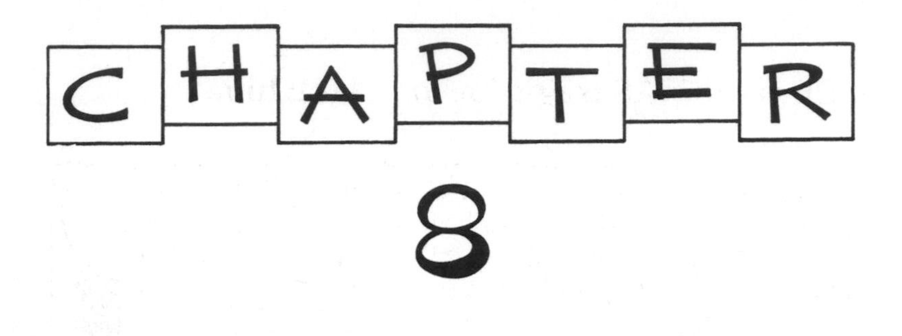

CHAPTER 8

"Well, this is a first," Francis says as we walk to school on Monday morning.

"What a tragedy," Teddy says. "For the gnome, I mean. Not for you."

"Oh yes it WAS tragic for me," I tell him.

Teddy cuts him off. "There ARE no interesting facts about lawn gnomes," he says. Then he points at a group of kids crowding around the bulletin board.

"Ooh!" Francis says, perking up. "They must have posted the Math Olympiad roster!"

There's actually something called the MATH OLYMPIAD? Sounds thrilling. What's next, a school punctuation team?

We elbow our way over to the bulletin board.

"So's Artur," notes Teddy.

"And so am I," says an obnoxiously familiar voice.

Oh, brother. Doesn't Gina ever get sick of patting herself on the back all the time?

"This is going to be SO much fun!" she exclaims.

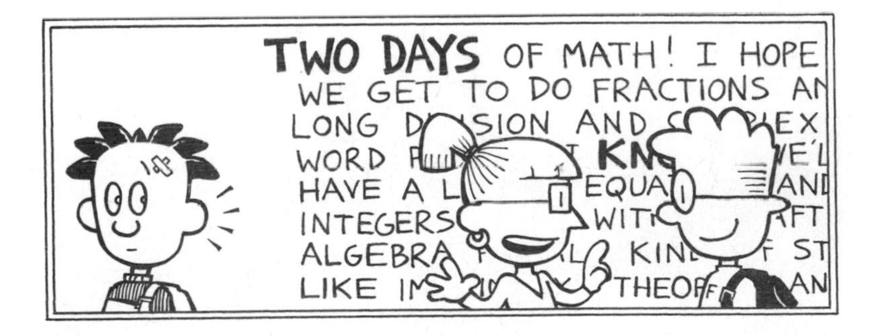

Huh? Two days? For the first time in her life, Gina just said something interesting.

"When IS this thing?" I ask.

"The Olympiad? This weekend," Gina says.

I don't even try to think of a snappy comeback. Did you hear that? THIS WEEKEND! That's PERFECT!

Francis chimes in. "It says here there'll be over FIVE HUNDRED kids competing!"

Normally, hearing about some humongous math meet would be about as interesting as watching Mrs. Godfrey bleach her mustache. But this is different. For TWO reasons:

See how it's all falling neatly into place? This is GREAT!

"Hallo, Nate," says a familiar voice.

"I hear you're going to the Math Olympiad this weekend, ol' pal!" I say, slapping him on the back. "You lucky duck!"

"Because you get to be teammates with GINA!" I say. "You two kids will be MAGIC together!"

Artur still looks confused. I'd better lay it on a little thicker.

"You know, I was Gina's partner last month for the social studies project," I say, putting a hand on Artur's shoulder.

"Nate," Artur says, "you are surprise me, the way you are talk about Gina."

Pretty smooth, right? Just call me Joe Cupid. If I keep planting these ideas in Artur's head, before long he and Gina will be on the express train to Togetherville.

And now, on to the next item on my list:

The whole odd jobs thing was okay, but it was a ton of work. And I obviously don't want a repeat of the lawn gnome fiasco.

Mrs. Godfrey looks mad—hey, THERE'S a surprise—and she's waving a piece of paper at me.

"This homework you handed in is COVERED with DOODLES!" she barks.

The idea hits me even before she's done talking.

I'll make my own comic book! That'll be WAY easier to sell than some stupid wall hanging. And here's the best part: Most of the work is DONE already! I draw comics ALL THE TIME!

For the rest of the day, I can't think about anything except my new business plan. At last bell, I don't wait for Francis and Teddy. I run home, zip up to my room, and start putting together . . .

It'll have old favorites, like this:

He'll keep you in "STITCHES"!
DOCTOR CESSPOOL!
Doctor Cesspool is visited by the chief of surgery...
Cesspool, I've received a report that you've BOTCHED another operation!
Who, ME?
Dr. Arch Enemy
I'm SUSPENDING you from the hospital!
GASP! NO!!
You can't DO that! Have some COMPASSION! Have a... a...

Nurse, what's that red, pulsing thing called?
A heart, Doctor.
Nurse Maureen
Biology
Can you at LEAST tell me what I'm accused of?
Very well. BRING IN THE PATIENT!
THAT'S HIM!! This man is a total HACK!
During my tummy tuck, he attached my FOOT where my HAND should be! And VICE VERSA!

And I'll also sprinkle in some of my NEW creations, like this one:

Lights!... Camera!... LAUGHS!
MOE MENTUM,
HOLLYWOOD STUNTMAN!
One day on the movie set...
J.B., I can't do this scene!
What's the problem, Moe?
raging river
The pressure of being a stuntman is GETTING to me! I just don't think I can swim over that waterfall!
I... I've lost my nerve!
It's okay, Moe. I'm here. I'll help you.
ACTION!!
SHOVE!

A few minutes later...
Groan!... I DID it, J.B.!
I broke sixteen bones, punctured a lung, and had five heart attacks!...
...but it was WORTH it! I faced my fears and did the scene!
That's right, Moe. You did.
And it wasn't bad, for a first take.
First take?
This time, don't scream so loud.
THE END

And that's only a few pages' worth. The complete book will be a LOT longer. The question is . . .

I settle on a nice, round number: five dollars. If I sell twenty copies of "Nate's Comix Crack-Up," that's a hundred bucks. Which is enough to buy . . .

Hm. Twelve doesn't sound like all that many. Not when you consider what ARTUR'S done. But I'm sure I can sell way more than twenty comic books. I'll just START with twenty.

"Um, yes, please," I say. "How much would it cost to make twenty copies of my comic book?"

She takes it from me, counts the pages, and punches the buttons on her calculator.

I practically pass out. That's almost as much as I earned this weekend! I gulp. For a few seconds,

I almost bag the whole idea.

Then I remember how awesome my comics are.

I pull a wrinkled wad of bills from my pocket and carefully count out thirty-four dollars. It seems like an awful lot of money. Still, I've heard people say that you've got to spend money to make money.

They'd better be right.

Unless you're one of those pencil necks going to the Olympiad, you're probably like me: You try to avoid math at all costs.

Here's what I mean: Since I spent all that money at the copy shop, selling twenty comic books for five bucks apiece doesn't equal a hundred dollars anymore.

That's only enough to buy EIGHT wall hangings, not twelve. I need to do better than that to catch Artur. Maybe I should sell them for six dollars instead. Or seven. But will people pay that much for a comic book?

Gordie has an after-school job at Klassic Komix in the mall. He's also Ellen's boyfriend. Dude. What were you THINKING?

But except for his putrid taste in girlfriends, Gordie's cool. And he's a total comics expert. If anybody can answer a comic book question, he can.

"We just got the new issue of 'Femme Fatality,' and it's INCREDIBLE!" he says. "I saved you a copy."

"Thanks, but I'm not buying today, Gordie," I tell him.

"It's my own original comic book," I announce.

He flips through it. "Mighty impressive," he says approvingly.

He kind of grimaces. "I'm not sure, Nate. That's pretty steep for a self-published book."

"But it's a RIOT!" I point out. "Can't we put it on display and let the CUSTOMERS decide?"

Gordie disappears into the back room while I stay by the counter. Then I notice a guy over in the corner. A big guy. A big, HAIRY guy.

He's talking to himself as he pulls some books off the shelves. Okay, that's a little weird.

He's putting stuff in his bag!

I turn to look for Gordie, but I don't have to. He's already here.

"SHOPLIFTER?" Gordie repeats. "Nate, he wasn't—"

"Yes, he WAS!" I shout. "He was STEALING stuff! I watched him do it! I'm an EYEWITNESS!"

Gordie holds up his hand like a stop sign. "Nate," he whispers, "that's Wayne."

Boss? HIM? The guy who made a wrong turn at one million B.C.?

"He was just getting rid of some stuff that hasn't been selling," Gordie says quietly.

Whoops. MAJOR whoops. But how was I supposed to know that? You've got to admit, the whole thing looked pretty suspicious.

"Uh . . . sorry about that, mister," I say.

Captain Caveman looks like he's getting in touch with his inner Godfrey. What's he gonna do, pull out a dinosaur bone and club me over the head?

(And, yes, I KNOW cavemen and dinosaurs weren't alive at the same time. It's an EXPRESSION.)

He fishes into his pocket and hands me a five.

"Here," he says. "I'll buy one . . ."

Oh, come ON. I can't walk around ringing doorbells again. That takes too long. There's got to be a better way to find . . .

DUH! Earth to Nate: You're standing in the middle of a MALL! This place is jam-packed with people looking to buy quality merchandise!

And quality's my middle name!

"But you've never seen a comic book like THIS one before!" I say, shoving it into her hand.

She turns to page one and frowns.

"Doctor CESSPOOL?" she says. "What kind of a name is that for a doctor?"

She hands the book back. "A man with a foot where his hand should be isn't funny," she sniffs.

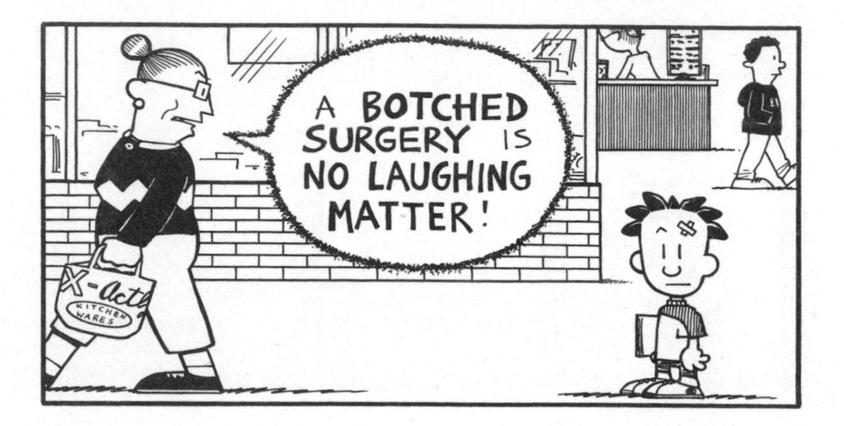

Wow. Speaking of surgery, can somebody give this lady a humor transplant? Lighten up, grandma.

I'll try Plan B.

"Check out this one!" I say, flipping the pages. "It's called 'Moe Mentum, Hollywood Stuntman!'"

The guy doesn't say anything; he just starts reading. I watch for a reaction.

Hel-LO? Is this dude even ALIVE? How could anybody read "Moe Mentum" without having some sort of . . .

Oops. Hold it. He's about to say something.

That's it? I offer him a chance to read a comic masterpiece, and all he can say is "I don't get it"?

There's a LOT that you don't get, pal. Exhibit A: You're wearing socks with your sandals. Which officially makes you a member of . . .

Obviously, my comics are too sophisticated for some people. Fine. Who needs 'em? There are plenty of other fish in the sea. I just need a way to reel 'em in.

That's IT! The perfect solution! Why talk to one customer at a time . . .

TESTING! 1...2...3... TESTING!
LISTEN UP, FOLKS! DO YOU LIKE COMICS? THEN GET YOUR BUTT OVER TO THE INFORMATION DESK AND BUY A COPY OF NATE'S COMIX CRACK-UP! NONSTOP LAUGHS! GUT-BUSTING GAGS! AND WHAT A BARGAIN! ONLY SIX DOLLARS!!
MAKE IT SEVEN AND GET YOUR COPY AUTO-GRAPHED!!
AHEM!
!

Uh-oh. Mall cop.

"What are you trying to pull, junior?" he asks angrily. He's breathing hard. He must have run all the way over here from the food court.

"Kid, you can't just walk in off the street and SELL stuff!" he sputters. "Not unless it's for some charity or school or—"

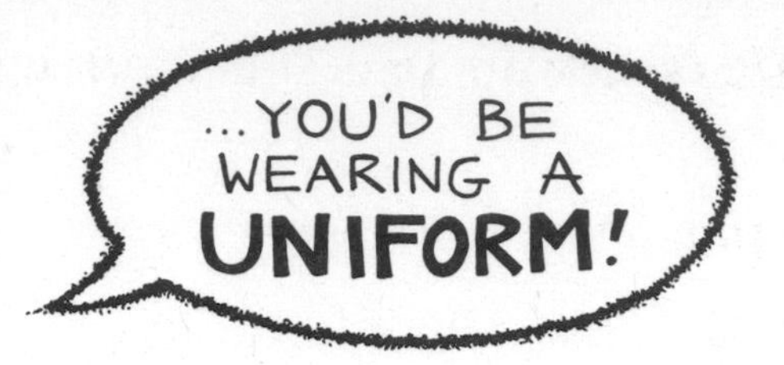

Gulp. Officer Friendly's got a point. And he's just getting started. He spends the next fifteen minutes going over all the important mall rules I've broken.

Finally, lecture time's over. He hands me a cell phone. "Call a parent to come get you."

For a second, I consider telling him I don't HAVE a parent. Being an orphan doesn't sound so bad right about now.

Don't pick up, Dad. Don't pick up. Don't . . .

"Hello?"

"Uh . . . hi, Dad, it's me," I say.

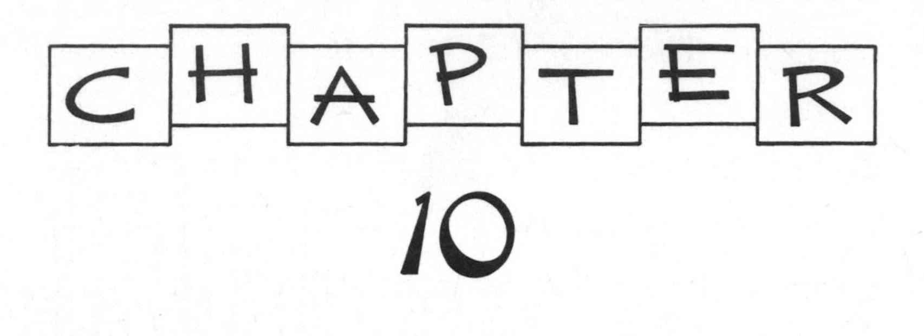

Ever been grounded?

It does in MY family, anyway. I know kids who get in trouble and they're all: "Ooh, my parents

GROUNDED me." But, EXCUSE me, they're still watching TV, talking on the phone, and using the computer. They can still DO stuff.

That's not how it is in OUR house. When Dad grounds me (notice I said "me" and not "us," because Ellen's NEVER been grounded), he doesn't mess around. There's no TV. No phone. No computer.

Dad doesn't see it that way. He says being grounded is an "opportunity." To do what—rearrange my sock drawer? I guess when you're Dad's age, sitting in your bedroom and slowly going bald is what passes for excitement. According to him, there's PLENTY to do when you're grounded.

SPYING ON YOUR SISTER!
You never know what you might find out... because older sisters lead such FASCINATING LIVES!!
...So then I changed into my PINK blouse, but it TOTALLY clashed with my skirt!
So I was like: "What'll I do?" And Debbie was like: "Let's text Amber! SHE'LL
What a RIVETING conver-sation!
PICKING LINT OUT OF YOUR BELLY BUTTON!!
I'll add this to my COLLECTION!
World Record Lint Ball →
HAVING FATHER-SON CHATS!
I'm grounding you for your OWN GOOD!
THANKS, Dad, for making me a BETTER PERSON!

Sounds fun, right? And being stuck here means I can't earn any money, either. So I haven't gained on Artur at all—not even while he was at that stupid Math Olympiad.

If Danny Discipline had only grounded me for a day or two, I'd have a better chance at that skateboard. But it's been a WEEK already! The only other time I've been grounded this long was that day I shaved Spitsy.

I still don't know what I did wrong. I mean, how ELSE was I going to get all that superglue off him?

Dad turns all serious on me when I come to the table. "Nate," he says, "provided you make it through school today with no INCIDENTS . . ."

YES! I'm FREE! Or I will be once school is over. I slam down my breakfast, brush my teeth, and grab my backpack.

Oops. I just remembered: Francis and Teddy went to school early this morning for BBC.

That stands for Breakfast Book Club. Hickey—Mrs. Hickson, the librarian—has BBC meetings every other Tuesday. Kids come in early to talk about whatever books they're reading, and Hickey serves apple juice and donut holes.

I'd be at BBC, too, if Dad hadn't thrown me in solitary. I wonder what I'm missing. I bet Amanda Kornblatt is talking about another horse book. If it doesn't say "pony" in the title, she . . .

Huh? Did they just say my name?

Okay, what's going on? Why's everyone talking about me? It can't be because of my little mall cop episode. That's old news by now.

I spot Teddy and Francis leaving the library. Forget telling them that I'm not grounded anymore; now I just want to ask them . . .

I'm getting annoyed. "What's so FUNNY?"

Say WHAT? LOVE BUNNY?? What am I—one of Ellen's stuffed animals? This can't be good.

"Your secret's out!" Teddy snickers. "You might as well admit it!"

The hallway starts spinning. "Are you INSANE?" I shout. "Gina's my WORST ENEMY!!"

"Not according to Artur!" crows Francis.

I feel like throwing up. You know what this means? Artur didn't get it. He was too clueless to realize I was trying to set him up with Gina.

And even worse: He BLABBED about it! Now everyone thinks I've got the hots for THE MOST OBNOXIOUS PERSON WHO EVER LIVED!! Hey, thanks a million, Artur.

The bell rings for homeroom, but I don't move. Do I really need to be in the same room with Artur and Gina right now? Maybe I'll just skip it.

But then I remember what Dad said at breakfast: that I'm not grounded anymore . . .

Skipping homeroom means detention. And detention is definitely an incident. Shoot.

I start toward Mrs. Godfrey's room.

Hickey's chasing after me, waving a piece of paper.

I recognize it right away. It's Artur's Warm Fuzzies order form. And it's PACKED.

I quickly scan it. Wow. He sold twenty on the first

day . . . fourteen the night of the "Peter Pan" show . . . then another three . . . then two . . . then five . . .

I add 'em all up.

Wait. How much? I knew Artur was selling his butt off, but THIS is RIDICULOUS. It feels like I just got punched in the stomach.

His eyes bug out. "THANKS you, Nate!" he says. "I was not even know I LOST this!" Then he lowers his voice to a whisper. "Now can you guess what nice something I did for YOU?"

He gives me a big smile and then nods like he's waiting for an answer. What does he expect me to say? I sure can't tell him the TRUTH.

"Forget about that whole thing, Artur," I say gruffly. "I like somebody else."

There. Was that simple enough for you? Maybe that'll put a stop to these ugly "Nate likes Gina" rumors.

Gina snarls at me like a rabid ferret. "I don't know what idiotic stunt you're trying to pull . . ."

I breathe a little sigh of relief. I mean, that's what I was EXPECTING her to say, but I was still sort of worried. What if THIS had happened?

There. THAT shut her up. Now I can focus on making it through the day. I just keep repeating the same two words: NO INCIDENTS!

It's exhausting. Staying out of trouble for a whole day is harder than you think. I have a close call during gym. And another in science.

But I make it. The bell rings. It's official: I'm not grounded anymore.

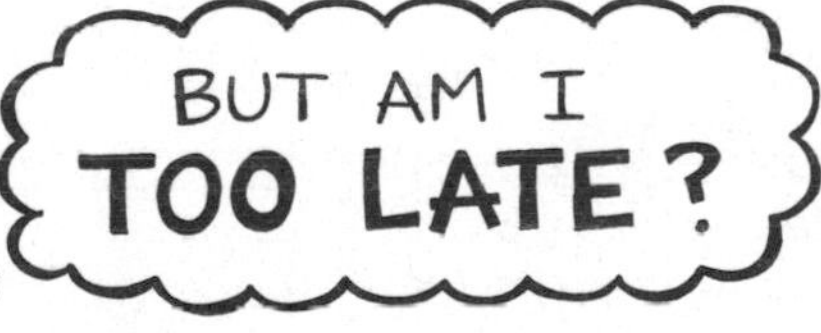

There's not much time. Our Warm Fuzzies orders are due at Thursday's troop meeting. I've got two days to catch up to Artur—if I can earn enough money.

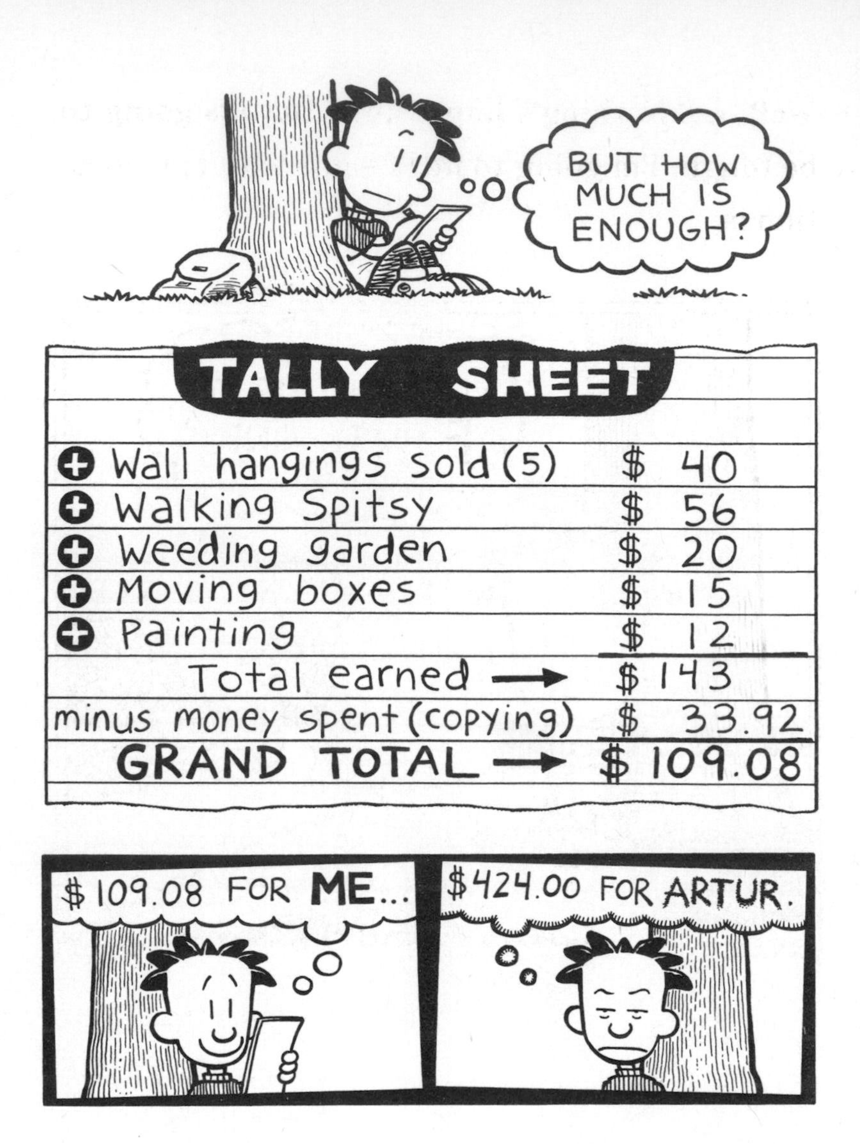

TALLY SHEET

⊕ Wall hangings sold (5)	$ 40
⊕ Walking Spitsy	$ 56
⊕ Weeding garden	$ 20
⊕ Moving boxes	$ 15
⊕ Painting	$ 12
Total earned →	$ 143
minus money spent (copying)	$ 33.92
GRAND TOTAL →	**$ 109.08**

Bottom line: He's way ahead of me. To win that skateboard—and to make Artur finish SECOND for once in his stinkin' life—I've got to earn over three hundred dollars by Thursday. Impossible.

Well, no. Nothing's impossible. But it's going to be tough. I'm going to need a miracle. The question is . . .

CHAPTER 11

My cheeks start to burn. “Oh . . . you heard about that, huh?”

Gordie laughs, but not in a mean way. “Nate, you hijacked the public address system!”

Exactly. I think I’m going to skip over that scene when I write my life story. Time to change the subject. “What’s that?” I ask.

“It lists the cash value of collectible comic books,” he explains, handing it to me. “You wouldn’t BELIEVE how much some of them are worth!”

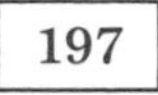

I flip through it. Hm. I thought I knew a lot about comics, but . . .

"Sure, Nate," he says. "Bring it down to the store later."

I sprint home.

Fast.

SKATEBOARD fast.

You're probably wondering what's going on. Well, I'm not really sure. Not YET. For now, all I can tell you is this:

It might be right under my nose!

At the end of the troop meeting on Thursday, we all give our order forms to Teddy's dad.

"Guys," Artur asks us, "what is jamboree?"

"It's sort of a Timber Scout carnival," Francis says. "Every troop in the city will be there."

"It's like the Math Olympiad, Artur," I explain.

There's Artur's ride. He waves as he climbs into the car. "Well, I hope I will winning a prize!" he says. "So longs, guys!"

"He HOPES he'll win?" Teddy wonders aloud. "The way Artur's been selling those wall hangings . . ."

"Don't be so sure, boys," I say. "Artur just might have some COMPETITION!"

"I WAS." I nod.

The guys look confused. Hey, I can't say I blame them. I'd never heard of "Bumble Boy" EITHER . . . until that yard sale last fall.

"So you bought some moldy old comic book," says Francis. "What does that have to do with the fund-raiser?"

"Cool your jets, Francis, there's more to the story!" I say. I tell them about Gordie and his price guide.

I couldn't believe it: A THOUSAND BUCKS!! I was almost POSITIVE I had the exact same comic book in my closet. I just wasn't sure I could FIND it.

It took a whole lot of searching. But finally . . .

"BUMBLE BOY," issue #12!
It matched the price guide perfectly.
My fifty-cent comic book was a
COLLECTOR'S ITEM!!

"End of story," I say.

"No, Gordie's boss said it wasn't in mint condition," I say. "The cover was a little bit ripped . . ."

"But he still paid me a lot. MAYBE enough to win that skateboard."

"If a skateboard was what you wanted, you could have just BOUGHT one with the 'Bumble Boy' money," Teddy points out. "You didn't have to spend it all on wall hangings."

"But then I wouldn't have raised any money for the Timber Scouts," I remind him.

"Well, how much DID you raise?" Francis asks.

"I don't want to jinx it," I say.

On Saturday morning, Francis and I walk over to the football field where the jamboree is. After we find Teddy and the rest of the guys, we walk around and check everything out.

That's when Artur starts bugging me.

ZING!
Good one, Nate!
THUD!
YOUR turn, Artur!
Hokay!
ZIP!
Artur, you're supposed to throw UNDER-HAND!
CLANG!!
A RINGER!
AWESOME, Artur!
Was just a lucky throw!
You can say THAT again.
Look! Mini golf!

Watch and learn, fellas!
CLICK!
ARRGH! So CLOSE!!
Look out, Nate! ARTUR'S putting!
Oop! Too hard!
SMAK!
TONG!
CLUNK!
A HOLE IN ONE!
Artur, you're AMAZING!

See what it's like? Even when Artur has no idea what he's doing, everything goes his way. It's so . . .

Oops. That's the scoutmaster. This could be it.

Yup, this is it. My stomach starts doing flip-flops. I MIGHT have raised enough money to beat Artur. Then again, he could have sold a lot more Warm Fuzzies since I saw his order form on Tuesday.

And who knows? Maybe some kid from another troop sold more than BOTH of us.

"Third prize, a build-a-robot kit, goes to . . ."

Polite applause. Josh walks up front and collects his prize. I clap a few times. Or I THINK I do. I'm so nervous, I can't feel my hands.

"And now for the top two prize winners . . ." Pause.

"Artur Pashkov and Nate Wright, both of troop three! Please come on up, boys!"

Everybody's clapping. People are pushing us toward the podium. I feel numb. So that's what I get for chasing after Artur for two weeks? A TIE??

"Both these scouts sold FIFTY-EIGHT wall hangings! They EACH deserve the grand prize!" the scoutmaster announces as we reach the podium. "But there can only be ONE WINNER!"

What? Really? THAT'S how we're deciding who gets the skateboard? A coin flip between me . . .

Technically, I know I've got a fifty-fifty chance.

But it doesn't feel that way. Not against Mr. Lucky. It feels more like a one out of ten chance. Or one out of a HUNDRED.

The scoutmaster nods my way. "Call it, young man." And before I can even think about it, the coin's in the air.

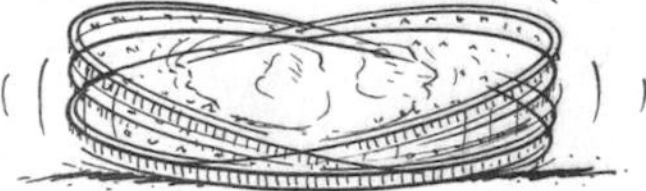

"Heads it is!"

Heads? So . . . I win?

"And Nate . . ." the scoutmaster says.

" . . . along with a certificate to have it custom painted at Ben's Board & Wheel!"

"Thanks," I manage to say, holding tight to the skateboard. MY skateboard. I can't stop staring at it. I guess Artur DOESN'T always win!

Suddenly he's right beside me. He holds out his hand. "Good jobs, Nate," he says.

I can't tell if he means it or not. See why Artur's so tough to figure out? He just lost something he tried really hard to win . . . but he still acts HAPPY for me. It's weird.

"I am invite all the guys to my house to set up my telescope!" he says.

"You go ahead, Artur," I tell him.

BIG NATE GOES FOR BROKE IS NEXT!
TURN THE PAGE FOR A SNEAK PEEK!

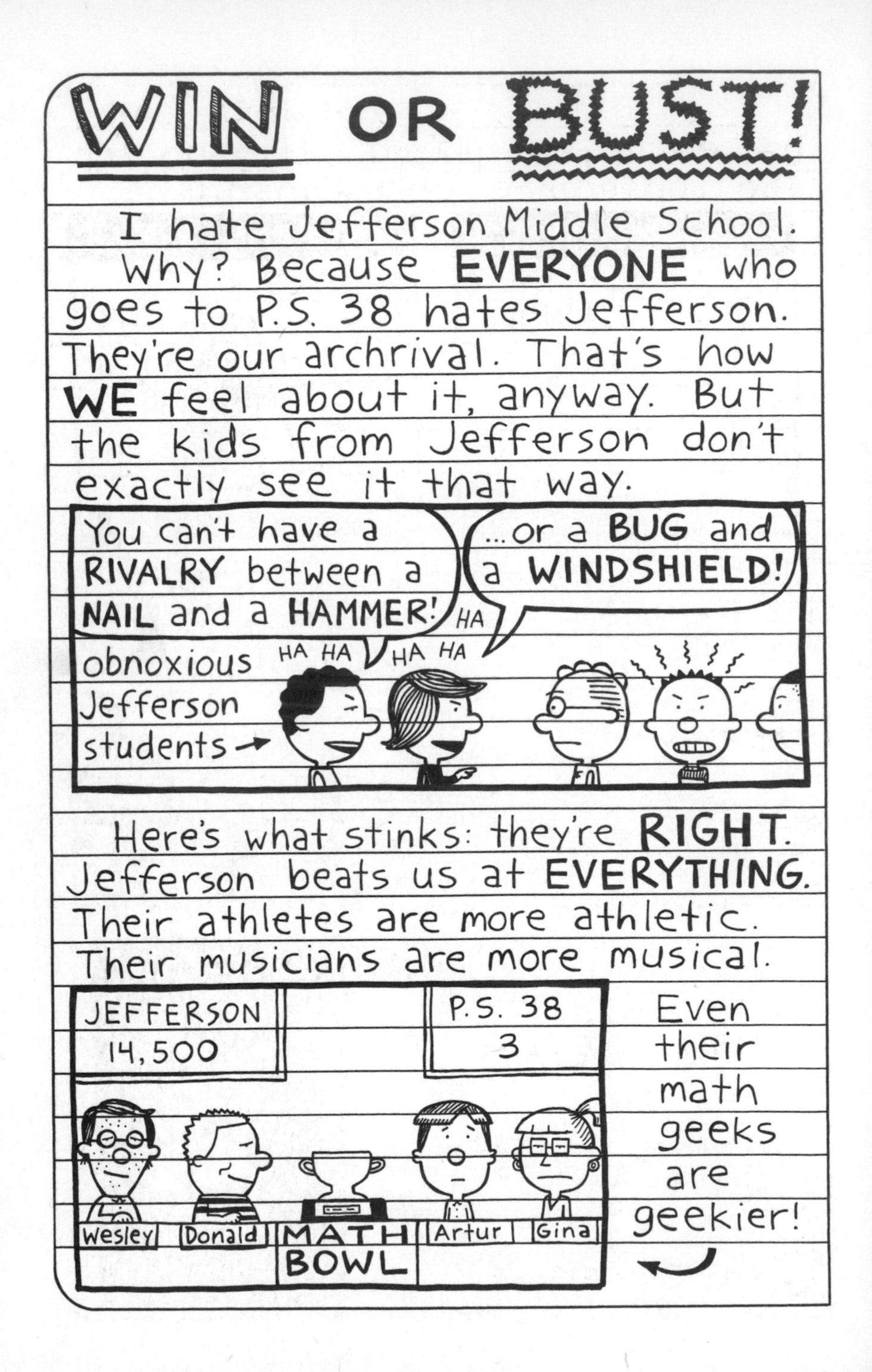
WIN OR BUST!
I hate Jefferson Middle School.
Why? Because EVERYONE who goes to P.S. 38 hates Jefferson. They're our archrival. That's how WE feel about it, anyway. But the kids from Jefferson don't exactly see it that way.
You can't have a RIVALRY between a NAIL and a HAMMER!
...or a BUG and a WINDSHIELD!
HA HA HA HA HA HA HA
obnoxious Jefferson students
Here's what stinks: they're RIGHT. Jefferson beats us at EVERYTHING. Their athletes are more athletic. Their musicians are more musical.
JEFFERSON 14,500
P.S. 38 3
Wesley
Donald
MATH BOWL
Artur
Gina
Even their math geeks are geekier!

The last straw was when our basketball team played Jefferson for the conference championship.
PRE-GAME SPEECH
We can BEAT these guys! I KNOW we can!
Coach Calhoun
POST-GAME SPEECH
Losing by 53 points really isn't all that bad.
A lot of people think we'll NEVER find a way to beat Jefferson. But not me. I've come up with a brilliant idea...
...and Jefferson won't know what HIT them!
J
What's my plan? Read BIG NATE GOES FOR BROKE to find out!
"Big Nate is funny, big time."
Jeff Kinney, author of Diary of a Wimpy Kid
BIG NATE
GOES FOR BROKE
Lincoln Peirce

Lincoln Peirce

(pronounced "purse") is a cartoonist/writer and the author of the *New York Times* bestsellers *Big Nate: In a Class by Himself*, *Big Nate Strikes Again*, *Big Nate Boredom Buster*, and the collections *Big Nate: From the Top* and *Big Nate: Out Loud*. He is also the creator of the comic strip *Big Nate*. It appears in over two hundred and fifty U.S. newspapers and online daily at www.bignate.com. *Big Nate* was selected for *Horn Book Magazine*'s Fanfare List of Best Books of 2010 and BarnesandNoble.com's Top Ten. Also, *Big Nate* will be published in nineteen countries, including Brazil, Canada, China, the Czech Republic, Denmark, France, Germany, Greece, Holland, Indonesia, Israel, Italy, Japan, Poland, Portugal, Romania, Spain, Taiwan, and Turkey, and will be translated into twenty languages.

Check out Big Nate Island at www.poptropica.com. And link to www.bignatebooks.com for games, blogs, and more information about the Big Nate series and the author, who lives with his wife and two children in Portland, Maine.

HEY, TIMBER SCOUTS! If nobody's buying those lame WARM FUZZIES, try selling BIG NATE'S COOL BUZZIES!
CARTOONING
"DRAWS" ME IN!
MATH
I ♥ U
CHEEZ DOODLES
LIBRARIANS:
PFFFT!
SILENT but DEADLY
P N A T E C
W R F L M S
S E O G N B
U H T C A L
I E W Y K R
L U B M D S
GET "BOARD"!